Battle of the Bands

Battle of the Bands

K.L. Denman

orca soundings

ORCA BOOK PUBLISHERS

Library and Archives Canada Cataloguing in Publication

Denman, K.L., 1971-
Battle of the Bands / K. L. Denman.
(Orca soundings)

ISBN 10: 1-55143-674-4 (bound) ISBN 1-55143-540-3 (pbk.)
ISBN 13: 978-1-55143-674-6 (bound) ISBN 13: 978-1-55143-540-4 (pbk.)

I. Title. II Series.
PS8607.E64B38 2006   JC813'.6   C2006-903259-9

First published in the United States, 2006
Library of Congress Control Number: 2006928471

Summary: The Lunar Ticks are on their way to the top.

MIX
Paper from
responsible sources
FSC
www.fsc.org
FSC® C016245

*Orca Book Publishers is dedicated to preserving the environment and has printed
this book on paper certified by the Forest Stewardship Council®.*

Orca Book Publishers gratefully acknowledges the support for its publishing
programs provided by the following agencies: the Government of Canada
through the Canada Book Fund and the Canada Council for the Arts,
and the Province of British Columbia through the BC Arts Council
and the Book Publishing Tax Credit.

Cover photography by Getty Images

ORCA BOOK PUBLISHERS
PO Box 5626, Stn. B
Victoria, BC Canada
V8R 6S4

ORCA BOOK PUBLISHERS
PO Box 468
Custer, WA USA
98240-0468

www.orcabook.com
Printed and bound in Canada.

14 13 12 11 • 7 6 5 4

*For Neil, the one who brings
people together.*

Chapter One

The smell in the garage is lousy. No matter how much incense Cia burns to cover it up, the aroma of mold and car exhaust lingers. Old bulbs coated with years of dust and cobwebs don't cast the best light either. But when I pick up my guitar and my fingers find the strings and that first riff comes screaming out of the amp, the only thing that matters is sound.

Kel joins in on bass and then Cia gets going, pounding out the beat, making snarly faces because she thinks drums ought to lead off. The girl does set down a solid rhythm, but I keep telling her, original doesn't follow any rules. Kel and I grin at her and she scowls. Then she smiles too and we get in sync, start gelling.

Sometimes that whole rush of being perfect lasts for all of two minutes and then one of us messes up and it's over. I say, *Man*, and Kel says, *Crap*, and Cia says nothing, just rolls her eyes. Then we go again. We keep going because, someday, everyone's going to listen to The Lunar Ticks.

That's us, our band. Kelvin is on bass guitar. He is over six feet tall, and on a lucky day, after pizza, he might weigh 130 pounds. His hair is long and thin too, and his feet! Let's just say his parents have his shoes special ordered.

They look like modified skis. The only wide thing on Kel is his mouth, and maybe that's what attracted his girl-friend, Amy.

Almost everything on Amy is wide. Her bottom end has a hard time staying inside the confines of her jeans—it's like she's oozing out everywhere. Her chest is mega, and then there's her mouth. It's not just the actual size, it's what she does with it. Her mouth is one of the band's main problems. She talks way too much, and every time we finish a song she has to plaster her lips to Kel's. Our practice time is seriously shortened by all the breaks for mouth to mouth. It's like some sort of lifesaving routine, and it's not pretty. I try not to watch, but sometimes I still catch a glimpse and it's scary. Scary because Amy's eyes are usually wide open and glaring at Cia.

Cia never watches the face-sucking act. She either keeps her sticks tapping or she lights up a cigarette and stares at the smoke drifting into the rafters. This leads to more delays. There's scenario *A*, in which we have to wait for Cia to finish her smoke, or scenario *B*, in which Cia's mom smells the smoke and starts yelling. I hate scenario *B*. It goes like this:

Alicia Stanton, what is that revolting stink? I'm going to count to ten and then I'm coming into that garage and all of your guests had better be gone because you are in trouble, young lady! Do you hear me? You are in deep trouble.

So then Mrs. Stanton starts counting, and Kel and Amy and I have to grab our stuff and make a run for it because if we don't make it out in time, we're in for a long lecture. We have to hear about how we ought to thank our lucky stars that she lets us kids use her garage for practice. We ought to be more considerate. Don't we know how bad smoking is for our health?

Cia never says a word. She just keeps staring at the rafters as her mom rages on. The funny thing is that Mrs. Stanton never blames Cia directly. Don't ask me why. It's not like Cia is the picture of sweet innocence. She has shorter hair than Kel or me, a spiky mix of purple, green and black. She has too many piercings to count. There's hardware in her nose, her lips, her eyebrows, her ears and who knows where else. I figure Mrs. Stanton knows it's Cia who smokes, but she pretends it's us so she can get her message across. Something twisted like that.

And then there's me, Jay. I'm not exactly perfect either, but I'm the leader of The Lunar Ticks. I'm the guy who got us together. We're a dedicated band. We have to be, because now is the time if we're ever going to be big. One day soon we're going to win a major battle, like the one coming up in June. It's just a couple of weeks away, and we need that win. The prize is an entire day in a professional recording studio. We're going to send out copies of our shiny CD, and all the DJs are going to play it and everyone's going to love it. We've got it all planned.

Chapter Two

Life outside the band is mostly boring. My parents aren't too harsh, and they did buy me my Gibson guitar. They got it secondhand, but it's a beauty with a flamed maple top and a tiger green nitrocellulose finish. It has a sweet rosewood fingerboard, and a mahogany body that fits me like it was made for me. Once in a while I play for my folks, and my mom puts on this bright little smile, nods and says, "That's great, Jay."

My dad squints and tries to find the rhythm with his fingers tapping the table, says he wishes he'd learned to play. And that's about all I have to do to keep them happy.

That, plus keep curfew and go to school, although grade eleven isn't my favorite gig. The other thing my parents do is keep a five-dollar bill taped to the door of the fridge. It got stuck there when they said I had an attitude problem back in grade ten. It came with the message, *If you don't want to follow the rules, there's your one-way ticket out of here, Jay.*

How far am I going to get on five bucks? I'm not stupid. I do what I have to do, be a regular guy who lives with a regular family in a regular house in the suburbs of Vancouver. If there's an upside to school, it's the band battles we have at lunchtime. Every couple of months we get to set up in the gym and go at it. Lately, we've won every time. Which leads me to another upside of school. The girls seem to like musicians. I get a fair bit of female attention. Okay, so maybe that isn't a good thing. I know I shouldn't complain, but it seems like a lot of those girls are like Amy. Pushy types who probably have way more experience than me.

Experience. That's my biggest problem. I just don't have enough experience in anything, and I consider this a flaw. How's an average guy like me supposed to come up with good music material when I haven't done anything yet? Sometimes I think I ought to take that five bucks and go, just hit the streets and find out what life is really about. It sucks to be stuck in kidville.

Today, Kel and I are headed for the music store. We won't be able to buy anything, but we go there just to pick out what we're going to buy when The Lunar Ticks make it big. It's like a ritual, same thing every time. We pause before entering the store, scan the display window, draw out the moment. Then we walk in and Kel forgets to breathe. He forgets to drop his backpack at the sales counter. He forgets that he usually trips over his ski feet when he moves too fast. It's like his brain is erased every time he enters the presence of the Fender Precision bass with sunburst finish.

Once we're standing in front of that glass case, Kel always whispers, "It's still here."

He puts his nose within a hair of the glass and drinks in every shiny, sexy curve of that guitar. His long face actually gets longer as he gazes, probably because his mouth hangs open.

I figure he's hearing Roger Waters from Pink Floyd laying down the bass line for "Money" on his Sunburst Fender. I swear, if Kel ever starts drooling, I'm going to hit him.

"Yeah," I say. "There it is." I don't know what will happen to him if someone else buys the Fender. He'll probably keel over on the spot. I hope that day never comes.

A tinny bit of a Green Day tune breaks the spell this time. Kel startles and his nose bumps the display case, marking it with a smudge. Then he digs in his pocket for his cell. "Hey," he croaks. His voice isn't back to normal yet.

"Where are you?" The shrill demand comes from Amy. I wouldn't be surprised if everyone in the store can hear her screeching over the phone.

"Down at the music store. With Jay."

"What? I thought you were coming over to see me! You promised, Kel."

"I did?" says Kel. He sounds truly surprised. He probably did agree to be there when Amy asked him over, but I know he tunes her out and just says yeah, yeah, yeah while she goes off. Can't say I blame him.

Still, it's not my problem. I leave Kel stuttering into his phone and head over to the amps. I could use a new amp. It's not that there's anything wrong with the one I've got, but I'd love to have one that puts out more distortion. Some of the tube amps are fantastic for producing some really wild stuff. I figure we could use some wild.

I'm studying the specs on a very fine, very expensive amp when I become aware of someone else across the aisle doing the same thing. Usually I wouldn't notice the other dreamers, but it's like some kind of crazy feedback loop starts a reverb in my gut, and I look up and there she is. Smooth pale skin.

Silky black hair. Long legs in tight black jeans. Her.

I don't know her, not really, but I do know this. Her name is Rowan, and she plays lead guitar in a band that's beat us in every battle outside the school. Her band is Indigo Daze and they are good. Really good. And she's really hot.

Rowan must feel me looking because her head snaps up and she nails me with a clear blue stare. A flicker of recognition dances across her face and she smiles, this tiny lift of the lips that makes me wonder. Is she mocking me? I can't tell, and that makes me mad. Or nervous. Or something. My first impulse is to smile back, but then I just drop my eyes and turn away like nothing happened.

And the moment's gone because here's Kel saying, "Hey, man, I've gotta go."

Chapter Three

When you're experience deprived, you should do something about it, right? Especially if you happen to be a creative type, like me. I've tried a couple of the obvious things other kids around here do when they want some excitement. Drinking, smoking weed. Remember that "attitude problem" back in grade ten and the five dollars on the fridge?

Let's just say I never got too far with the obvious stuff. Not only did it get me grounded for a month, but it didn't give me anything unique or real. It just got me sick or high, like everyone else.

Maybe I wouldn't feel like I need to live more if it weren't for Kel and Cia depending on me. When we first got together and formed the band, I came up with some good lyrics for a song, and ever since they've expected more. I have to admit it feels good to have their admiration, but that's also a lot of pressure.

So here's what I do. On the night of the full moon, I go looking for life. I know that sounds lame, but I've heard that people get crazier when the moon is full, so chances of finding something cool must be good. Plus I needed something that would keep me on a routine. The moon is on a routine, right? It fit. Nobody knows I do this, nobody.

I tell my folks I'm spending the night at Kel's, and Kel covers for me and that's it. Kel has asked what I'm up to, but I just shake my head and say, "It's about the art, okay?" That always shuts him up. He just doesn't know what to say.

Okay, he does look at me like I'm the Precision Fender and says, "Solid, man."

The first time, I spent the night in a graveyard. It was freaky, but I got a decent song out of it. It's called "You're Dead," and it goes like this:

Rotten bones
Cold in the dirt
Your face has gone away.
And if I try
I might see you
Too bad there's only one way.
You're dead, you're dead, you're
   dead!
(we scream that chorus line)

Never thought you'd go
Didn't want you to
And now you creep me out.
Our time is done
I want to puke
You know what I'm talkin' about.
You're dead, you're dead, you're
  dead!
Dark in the crypt
My eyes weep blood
Did you go to hell?
If we meet again
Don't call my name
Cuz then I'll know I fell.
You're dead, you're dead, you're
  dead!

Not bad, eh? A tune like that has a double meaning. It could be about a relationship breakup, or it could be about a dead person. The audience can figure it out whichever way they like.

The truth is, the graveyard mostly made me sad. There was this one grave with white daisies on it. The marker said *Farewell darling angel. Willow Ann Raynor.* She was sixteen when she died. The same age as me.

Another time I went and hung out at the Skytrain station. I planned to just sit on a bench in a dark corner and watch for action, but it was cold that night so I ended up walking up and down the platform to keep warm. This old scruffy guy started walking with me, talking at the speed of Amy. He made about as much sense as Amy does too, and he smelled really bad, like old beer. He was telling me about this vegetable garden he used to have with beans and Walla Walla onions, whatever those are. I wanted to tell him to take off, but I didn't. I was actually hoping he'd get around to saying something interesting. He never did.

I finally said, "Buddy, what is your problem?"

And then the old guy starts to laugh, and the next thing he's crying, so I put my hand on his shoulder. Right then a train pulls up and this group of girls gets off. They start staring at me like I'm some psycho, and one of them says, "What are you doing to that old man, you loser?"

Another one of the girls whips out her cell and says, "I'm calling the cops."

I say, "Hey, I didn't do anything to him," and they say, "Yeah, right!" and the old guy starts to sob even louder. He chokes out, "I want my onions back." The girls look really confused, and I do the only thing I can think of. I pull out my wallet and give him my last twenty bucks and say, "Fine. Go get some."

He stops crying. He stares at the bill for half a second, says, "Thanks, kid, I'll have one for you," and off he goes.

The girls start laughing, and me, I leave, fast. I still haven't got a song out of that one.

It'll be better next time. I'm planning to hang around Vancouver's Downtown Eastside. Scarier than the graveyard, but I'm a decent-size guy in pretty good shape. And I'm desperate.

Chapter Four

"Don't do a Don!"

That's our band motto. Cia, Kel and I are warming up for a gig in the gym, and when Cia hisses those words, we all relax a little. We used to have a fourth member, Don, on keyboards. Every time we tried to perform, he froze. It really sucked, but the last time he played with us, he decided to do something about it.

He grabbed the mike, put it to his butt and let one rip. I figured he must have flipped out, but he said no. He just knew he couldn't take the pressure and decided to end his music career on a memorable note.

I guess our motto is a tribute to Don.

We were mad at him for a while because the teachers banned us from the next battle, but we're okay with him now. He's one of our biggest fans, and he always helps get the crowd howling for us.

This is our last performance before the big one coming up next week at the youth center. We've decided this will be like an omen for that show, and we plan to really rock today. Three other bands have already played, and we're the last ones. Going last can be a bonus. The crowd is already warmed up and ready for more music. Another plus is the kids will usually keep cheering if they think they'll get a longer lunch hour out of it.

"Ready?" I ask.

"Lunar Ticks!" someone screams from the floor. It's Amy, already bouncing around at the front of the crowd. I'm distracted because it looks like she forgot to wear a bra, and I miss my cue for the opening number. That chick is such a pain.

I mutter, "Sorry," to Cia and Kel. Then we start over and it's perfect. I don't think the crowd even noticed that Cia had to play her setup twice. That's the great thing about music. It can flow, just be a jam session where nothing is planned. Sure, you have to be ready, and maybe we aren't quite good enough yet to just let anything happen in a performance. Even the pros can't do much of that because the fans always want to hear the hit songs, right?

We blast our way through the first two numbers and then it's time for our final song, "You're Dead." We've only played it in public once before and it wasn't too polished then, but this time we nail it. The gym goes nuts. They love us!

It takes a while for the vice-principal to settle things down. He makes the usual threat that the school day will be extended to make up for missed time. Nobody actually believes him because there's no chance the teachers will agree to work longer, but we go along with him just in case. Then he calls the bands out onto the stage again, one by one. The crowd decides who wins by clapping and cheering the loudest and longest for their favorite. Sometimes it's hard to call the winner, but today there's no doubt. The Lunar Ticks score.

There are two long periods of classes to get through before we can gather in Cia's garage after school, but once we're there, it's celebration time.

"Were we awesome or what?" Kel says.

"You were awesome!" Amy tells him. Then, of course, she has to plaster her big lips on his.

"It was cool," Cia murmurs. "Way cool."

Amy comes up for air and sneers, "Yeah, but no thanks to you, Cia! You screwed up."

"Whoa," I say. "What are you talking about?"

"She was off right from the start. She couldn't wait to be first, like always. Lucky for her, nobody noticed. But I did."

"Hey," Kel mumbles. "That's not what happened."

Amy draws away from Kel and plants her hands on her hips. "Damn right that's what happened, Kel! Why are you defending her?"

"Amy," I say. But before I can explain, she cuts in.

"Cia's your biggest weakness, you know. She isn't good enough. If The Lunar Ticks are ever going to be great, you're going to have to ditch her and you know it."

Cia sucks in a breath and spits back, "What do you know? You're just a dumb groupie bitch."

Amy's hand snakes out like she's going to hit Cia, but Kel catches her arm. I've never seen him so red in the face before. He glares at Amy and growls, "Stop it!"

"What do you mean?" Amy squawks. "You're not going to let her get away with that, are you? You know I'm right. I've told you tons of times before, she's no good."

A muffled little noise comes out of Cia's throat and then she's gone, slamming through the door into the house.

"Amy," Kel says very quietly, "get out."

"What?" Amy's eyes narrow to slits. "What did you say, Kel?"

"I said get out. I've had it with you. We're through."

Amy grabs hold of his sleeve and tries to get her mouth near his face, but he pushes her away. "I mean it, Amy. Screw off."

"But, Kel!" she wails.

And Kel strides away, goes through the door Cia took. He slams it so hard that Cia's cymbals shiver out a chime from their stand.

Amy looks at me, and I guess she doesn't find what she's hoping for in my face. She gives a little sniff, goes over to the door, kicks it and screams,

"Bastard!" Then she spins around, marches past me again and she's gone.

This wasn't exactly what I had in mind for celebrating our win today, but all things considered, I don't think it turned out too bad.

Chapter Five

Things seem okay with Cia. I don't
know what Kel said to her, but when we
meet for our next practice she grabs her
sticks and starts drumming the way she
always has—totally excellent. I have
to admit that when it comes to sheer
skill on an instrument, Cia is the best
in our group. I watch her for a minute.
Sometimes you get so comfortable with

a person you don't really look at them anymore. They're just there. Cia isn't what I'd call pretty or cute, but she is sharp. She has a certain style of her own that goes beyond punk. Maybe it's the way her big brown eyes study the world and don't get hard or bored. Or maybe it's that grace she has in her body, probably from drumming. I think the job of keeping the beat has worked its way right inside her. She's not my type for a girlfriend, but I really care about her.

"What are you staring at?" she snaps. She's still a tough chick.

"You," I say. "You're damn good, you know."

"Shut up," she says, but she's smiling.

"All right," I say. "Game on." And we go. And go. No Amy delays, no smokes, no Mrs. Stanton kicking us out. It's amazing. We push on and sweat starts running down my back and still we play. The tips of my fingers are numb when we reach a point that feels like a wall. I lean into my guitar, feel Kel practically vibrating beside me, look across to see Cia biting down on her lip. A feedback loop I've never heard before comes sliding out of the amp and we all snap our heads up, meet each other's surprised faces, keep going. We're all grinning like fiends now, and then there's one more riff, a low line of bass from Kel, a fade-out roll from Cia and we're done.

Silence. No, not quite. There's us breathing like we just ran a mile. It's as if we're all afraid to speak and break the spell. What we just did was magic.

Kel's the first to comment. He puts his fingers in his mouth and whistles, sharp and loud.

"Too right," I say and slap him on the shoulder.

"Cool," Cia adds.

"You know what?" I ask. I don't wait for an answer. "We're going to win that battle next week. We're finally gonna be on our way."

Cia wrinkles her nose. "You think?"

"Yeah, I think."

"What about Indigo Daze?" Kel asks. "They'll be there."

"Don't worry about them. They're not going to beat us this time."

Kel shakes his head. "How can you be so sure?"

"Cuz I am," I say quietly. "If we can play like this…"

"You don't think this was a fluke?"

"Kel, my man, you have to believe me. Tell you what, though. I happen to know that Indigo Daze is playing in their school battle tomorrow. Want to go check them out?"

"How are we going to do that?" Cia asks.

"We go to their school at lunchtime and we just mingle with the crowd and that's it. Simple."

Cia looks doubtful. "We'll miss class. If I get caught skipping again, my mom will ground me for life."

"So we won't miss class, okay? I'll get us a ride and we'll leave the minute lunch starts and be back by the time lunch is over. It's only five minutes away by car."

"Who's going to give us a ride?" Kel asks.

"Don. I figure he still owes us. He won't mind driving."

Kel grins, but Cia keeps frowning. "Isn't there some rule about how many passengers he can take with a new license?"

"Yeah, but it's a short drive, and a couple of us can lie down in the back-seat or something. It'll be okay."

And it is okay, at first. Don says no problem, he'll take us. Next day we go in his car, and we're at the other school in time for the first band's opening number. We spread out, try to act like we belong. A couple of kids give us sideways looks, but nobody asks us what we're doing there.

Me, I don't even pay attention to the other bands. They're bad. What I do is try to catch sight of Rowan. What is it about that girl? I should be cold toward her because she's like the enemy, but for some reason I just wish I could talk to her. I think I see her once. There's this flash of silky black hair on the far side of the gym and I crane my neck. But no. Suddenly I get a strange prickle down the back of my neck and I turn, and there she is.

Rowan is looking at me with that same little half smile she wore in the music store and there's this jolt in my gut.

She knows who I am, I can tell. This time I try to smile back. I feel like a little kid who's been caught doing some dumbass thing like passing a note in class. A note that says, *You're cute,* or something really lame like that.

She tilts her head to one side and I think she's going to say something, but then the crowd starts this chant, "Raynor! Indigo! Raynor!" Rowan looks startled, but then she's gone, slipping away like water through fingers.

Raynor? What does that mean? And why does it sound so familiar? I don't have time to figure it out, not totally, because there she is on stage. Her guitar is hugged close to her body and, damn, I'm jealous of a guitar! The crowd is still chanting, "Raynor! Indigo! Raynor!" When Rowan puts up her hand and everyone cheers, I get it. They're calling her Raynor. Duh. That's her last name. So she's Rowan Raynor. Something else about that still bugs me, but when she lays into her guitar, a Gibson Firebird, and the sound comes alive, I forget about that. I just listen.

That girl can play. Her fingers dance over the strings so swift and easy I'm hit with an image of leaves in the wind. It looks so natural, so right. And then she starts to sing and her voice is like a comet flying, burning its way across the galaxy. Burning its way into me. I'm so into her color that I barely catch the words. Color? Yeah, the sound is like gold and purple, intense. She's singing about loss and goodbye and I feel sad, so sad I might start crying. How can she do that to me? I swallow and look around and everyone is caught in her fire. Some girls, guys too, have tears on their cheeks.

When the song ends I think it's time to get out of there. This was too much, too disturbing on every level. But then

Rowan is singing again and there's no way I'm leaving. I barely notice when Cia and Kel come up and start pulling me away. I'm outside, blinking in the sunshine, before I come back to the present.

"Hurry up, Jay! We're going to be late!"

"Huh?"

"Man, what's the matter with you? You look like you're high. You haven't been smoking up, have you?"

"What? No. What are you talking about?"

"Forget it. Let's just get in the car."

So we get in the car and we're almost back to our school when we get pulled over by a cop.

Chapter Six

The cop is wearing one of those rock-hard faces as he asks for Don's driver's license. Don is shaking and stuttering. We forgot about hiding in the backseat.

"You are aware that your novice license allows only *one* non-family passenger, are you not?" The cop's tone is nasty.

"Yessir. I am. I guess I forgot. It was just a short drive, doing a favor for my friends here…"

"Too bad your friends aren't doing you any favors." The cop shakes his head like he's disgusted.

"It's my fault," I blurt, but he cuts me off.

"Was I talking to you, mister?"

"No, sir."

"I didn't think so. Now you kids just sit right there. I've got some writing to do." He pulls out a pad of paper, slowly finds a pen and clicks it open. Then he fumbles around trying to open up the pad, rubs his hand along his jaw, stares off into space. We all slump down in our seats. We are so busted. This, plus there is no way we're going to be back at school on time.

When the cop is finally done writing, he informs Don that his license will be suspended for one month. The details about that will be sent by mail. Then he tells the rest of us to get out of the car. "Have a nice walk," he says.

Kel, Cia and I get out of the car. Don has his head down on the steering wheel. "Man," I say, "I'm really sorry. Really sorry, Don."

Don doesn't look up. He mumbles something I can't hear. I look at the cop, who has his arms folded across his chest, watching. "Please, officer. It was my idea. I asked him to do it and it was just a five-minute ride for…a school project."

The cop says nothing.

"It's not like he was speeding or anything. Don's a good driver, really careful. And I swear we won't ever do this again."

Still the cop says nothing. I feel like such a jerk. "Isn't there anything we can do?" I plead.

He laughs. Then, "Maybe there is something you can do. You seem sincere about this, and I'm in a good mood. How about you sing me a song and I'll let your buddy off with a warning."

He doesn't think I'll do it, I can tell. He figures maybe I'll just get mad and mouth him off or I'll slink away. But there's no way I'm going to let Don down, not if I can help it. I straighten my shoulders and take a breath.

Cia hisses, "Don't sing 'You're Dead'!"

She has a point. So what, then? And the next thing I know I'm singing, "The wheels on the bus go round and round, round and round…" The cop bursts out laughing. Kel, Cia and Don are all staring at me like I've lost it. I can't believe I'm doing this either, but I am. I get through the first verse, go into another one about the driver on the bus going up and down, and the cop starts waving his hands.

41

"Okay, okay. Enough." He turns to Don and says, "Would you mind handing me that notice?"

Don is grinning like a guy who just got away from a firing squad. When he gets the ticket back, he holds it up to show us. Written in large letters across the paper is the word *Warning*.

"Thanks, man," I say to the cop.

"Yeah, thanks a lot, officer, sir," Don says.

The cop gives him one more stare down. "It won't happen again, right?"

Don says, "Uh-uh, no way." And the cop gets back in his patrol car and that's that.

The other three turn and look at me.

"What?" I say.

"The Wheels on the Bus?" Kel snorts. Then they're all laughing.

"So I couldn't think of anything and then a bus drove by..." They aren't listening. They just laugh harder.

"Forget it," I tell them and start walking toward the school.

Kel and Cia follow behind, singing "The Wheels on the Bus" the whole way back.

Not that our troubles are over. We're late, and Cia's teacher is one of those who won't let anyone into class after the bell. Cia doesn't manage to be the one to answer the phone call to her house later that afternoon. Her mom gets the automated message. "Your son or daughter had one or more unexplained absences from school today. If you were not aware of this absence, please discuss this with your son or daughter."

So Mrs. Stanton discusses it by grounding Cia for two weeks.

"What are we going to do?" Cia moans.

"I don't know. Do you think your mom would listen to me if I talked to her?"

"I doubt it. But you can try. Maybe you could sing 'The Wheels—'"

"Shut up," I say. "That's not going to happen again. Ever."

"So what then? We're going to miss the battle?"

There is no way I want to miss the battle. Not this time. "You don't think you could sneak out?"

"Oh, yeah, right," she says. "I'm going to sneak out with a drum set."

"Okay. I guess I'll talk to your mom."

I bring Kel along for support, but he turns out to be pretty useless. He just sits on the couch in the Stantons' living room with his long limbs folded up in odd angles and says nothing.

"Hi, Mrs. Stanton." I pause and clear my throat. She's watching me like an ostrich. I once met this ostrich at a zoo, and it had a real mean stare. There were signs on the pen, *Warning! I Bite.* Trust me, you don't want to mess with an ostrich, but right now I have to. I say, "You know we've been working really hard to get ready for our next show."

Adults always like talking about hard work.

"If you call making a bunch of noise hard work, then I guess you've done that," she says.

Clearly, that line isn't going to do it. "Well, we really appreciate you letting us use your garage for practice."

Gratitude is good, right? They like that.

Mrs. Stanton rolls her eyes. "It's about time you kids showed some gratitude."

Wow, she's really tough. Cia must have got that from her.

"Oh, yes, ma'am. We are very thankful." Can I suck up, or what?

"If that were true, you wouldn't be smoking down there."

I blink a couple of times to make sure I don't look at Cia. "Well, Mrs. Stanton, I can promise you, we won't ever smoke in your garage again." Now I look at Cia. She sticks her tongue out.

Mrs. Stanton sniffs. "You're saying you promise?"

"Yes. For sure. We promise."

"Good. I'm going to hold you to it."

I think I've made some progress here. "No worries, Mrs. Stanton. The thing is, we were wondering if you might let Cia off her grounding for the night of the contest. Please. Just for that one night. It's really important."

Mrs. Stanton narrows her eyes. If we were in a Western movie right now, I'd be diving for cover. "Hmph. If it was so important, maybe Alicia should have thought of that before she cut class again."

"The thing is, that was a mistake. Sort of an accident. Cia wasn't trying to cut class, she was just a little late. And it was my fault. We got held up at lunchtime…"

"You got held up? What are you talking about?"

"I mean we were delayed. We were in this situation." I'm talking really fast now. "It's not important. But what I was thinking was maybe we could do something else to make it up."

"Like what?"

"Well, like maybe we could clean your garage for you."

I hear Cia and Kel gasp. I ignore them. I didn't warn them about this. It just came to me, in the moment.

Mrs. Stanton has a gleam in her eye. "You're willing to clean the garage? Really clean it?"

"You bet. We'll do a real good job."

She grins and looks at each of us, one by one. "It's a deal. You know, I might have let her off in exchange for weeding the flower bed. I do understand how much you kids want to win that contest."

Man.

Chapter Seven

"You and your big mouth, Jay." Cia isn't happy with me.

"Too right," Kel grunts. He's wrestling with a large hunk of plywood. We have to move it so we can get at the fifty cans of old paint we're supposed to haul away.

"What about the battle?" I ask. "We get to go, don't we?"

They don't say anything, not out loud. But Cia mutters stuff like, "Whatever. Could have been weeds. Way easier than this."

I ignore her. I have something else to think about while I operate a broom. I had this dream last night and I can't shake it. It was all mixed up, the way dreams are, but the part I remember most clearly is that I was a midget. Maybe a dwarf. Anyway, I was small but not a kid, and I was talking to a giant guitar. Then the guitar morphed into a skeleton and started laughing and chanting, "Raynor, Raynor." I woke up sweating and hardly slept again for the rest of the night.

What does it mean? Am I so spooked about how good Indigo Daze is that I feel like a midget compared to them? And why did the guitar turn into a skeleton? What's that about?

And then it hits me. The girl buried in the graveyard, her last name was

Raynor too. Just like Rowan's. I stand still to think about this. That sad song Rowan sang, about goodbye. The other kids in the gym crying. They knew. The song was about her sister dying.

I want to throw the broom across the garage and go find Rowan right now. I want to talk to her, tell her...What? That I understand? Only how can I really understand? Or maybe I do because she made me feel what she felt when she sang, didn't she? So that's what I should tell her, that she gave me something. How can a guy just come right out and say that to a girl? I could try. I could walk up to her and say I think she's really talented and maybe she and I could get together some time to talk about music. Then we'd go for coffee and sit beside each other in a booth and we'd connect...

"Hey, Jay. Are you going to sweep with that broom or make out with it?" Smart-ass Kel.

I swing around with the idea of pasting him with the broom, only I don't because there's Amy. She's standing in the doorway with her big lips pouting. She says, "Kel, babe? Can I talk to you for a minute?"

Kel ducks behind the plywood. I can't believe he did that. It only takes him a second to figure out that isn't going to work, because his long face shows itself again, bit by bit. First the forehead, then the eyes, followed by the nose and mouth. He keeps his chin hidden.

"Amy," he says. "No."

"What?" Amy whines. She takes a step forward.

"I don't want to talk to you. I'm busy."

"But Kel! It's important. I really need to tell you something."

Kel looks like he may be weakening. A wrinkle appears on his brow. But no, he's shaking his head. "Amy, I told you. We're done. End of story. There's nothing to talk about. And stop calling my house all the time. My mom's getting mad."

"So why don't you answer the phone sometimes?"

Kel just glares at her.

Amy starts pleading in this high-pitched voice. "Listen, Kel, it was all a mistake, okay? I didn't mean whatever I said. I think I was just PMSing, all right? You know I'd do anything for you, Kel. Just give me another chance."

This is embarrassing. I'd even feel sorry for Amy if I thought she meant what she was saying. Which I don't. I dart a glance at Cia and she's got ostrich eyes. Kel looks like he wants to hide behind the plywood again, but instead he steps right out. "Amy, I've heard all this before. You say crazy stuff, then you say you're sorry. I'm not falling for that again. Just get it through your head, it's over. Finished."

"Fine!" Amy hisses. "Have it your way, Kel. For now. But we are going to get back together. You need me too, you know!" She spins around and stomps out.

We're all breathing a sigh of relief when her head pops in again, like the creature in an *Alien* movie, scaring the crap out of us. "Just you wait and see!" she yells. Then her head snaps back out and we stand there, holding our breath.

Finally Kel says, "Is she gone?"

I inch toward the door and peer out. "All clear," I say.

"Man," Kel moans. "What did I see in her?"

"You're asking us?" Cia doesn't really expect an answer, but Kel gives her one.

"I wish someone would've told me."

"Told you what?" I ask. "That's not something anyone else can tell you about. Love is blind, right?"

"I never loved her," he says. "Okay, maybe I thought I did, for a while. But now I feel like an idiot. It's so obvious what a cow she is."

Cia pats his shoulder. "Don't worry about it, Kel. We're all human."

I don't tell them what I thought about Amy being an alien.

It takes our entire Saturday to clean that garage, but when we're done we have to admit, we like the results. It smells better for one thing. We found a big sack of rotten, moldy potatoes in one corner, and getting rid of them helped a lot. The light is better too. We discovered a window behind a bunch of old cardboard and cleaned it off. Actual sunlight comes into the place now. The last thing Cia does is dust off her drum set, and then she sits down and lays out a fast pattern, goes heavy on the bass and finishes with a cymbal crash.

"Hey, you know what?" Kel says. "I think the sound is better in here."

"Yeah," I say. "It does sound sharper."

Cia raises her eyebrows. "Are you kidding?"

And Mrs. Stanton is yelling, "That's too loud. Turn it down!"

Great. All the junk we took out must have been making a sound barrier. Shouldn't Mrs. Stanton know by now that there's no way to turn down drums?

"I think I need a cigarette," Cia sighs.

Chapter Eight

I go home and have a nice long shower, eat dinner, figure maybe I'll just take it easy tonight. The problem is, I can't stop thinking about Rowan. I feel like I'm obsessing. I have this horrible thought that maybe this is what Amy feels like. What if I turn into someone like her, get all clingy and crazy? How nasty would that be? I decide I better do something about this and call Kel to ask if he wants to see a movie.

"Can't," Kel says. "I have to babysit my little brother tonight."

I call Cia and she says, "Duh. I'm grounded, remember?"

I try Don, but he's already got plans. I even consider calling this girl from school who keeps hinting around that she'd like to go out with me. Then I get really brave and think, what the hell, why not call Rowan? So I look up her name in the phone book and there's the address too. She doesn't live that far away.

I could just go for a walk, couldn't I? It's not even dark yet when I set out. I love this time of year, early June, when the days are long and everything looks new. Lawns are still bright green and the air is fresh and soft. Another bonus is that summer is almost here. Sure, there are final exams coming up, but there are still a couple of weeks before I have to worry about studying. No point in stressing over stuff like that too soon.

Summer is going to be good. Lots of sleeping in, beach parties, waterskiing at the lake, maybe some gigs. Maybe a day in a recording studio? Yeah, if we win the battle next Saturday night, that's the prize. I wonder how many tracks we'll get to record? If it's more than two, we've got a problem. We only have two original songs and one of them is kind of bad. I need to come up with a new song.

That's what I should be doing, working on a tune or lyrics or both. I've got to find some raw material. I stop and look around, see a cat scurrying across the road.

Run, cat, run, go catch your meal.
Eating to live is a really big deal.

Meh. What else? I look up and there's a jet cruising overhead. Think, Jay, think. Let's see. Nope. Nada. Zip. No new song. Instead I wonder where those people are going. Wonder if there's a terrorist on board who will blow them out of the sky. What is with those terrorist losers anyway? What does it prove, blowing stuff up? It just makes the rest of us think they're totally bent. So maybe they have some kind of cause, but who wants to listen to crazy killers? I mean, I can see where they might have some problems with the way things are. Who doesn't? But killing people because of that?

I'm not exactly happy with every-thing myself. I think the way the world runs is rotten in a lot of ways. So many people want to tell you how to live your life. Rich people are getting richer on the backs of the poor, making kids work in factories. Imagine that, little kids in Third

World countries working all day for almost nothing, making stuff like runners.

Who told me about that? My humanities teacher? It's bad news because I'm looking at my feet and there's a pair of runners. They're pretty nice ones too, a popular brand. Damn. I sit down with my back against a tree and pull off my shoes. I'm checking them out, wondering about how they were put together, when someone says, "Are you stalking me or what?"

It's Rowan. I gape at her for at least ten seconds and then say, "Huh?" So lame.

"I asked if you're stalking me."

She's sure got a high opinion of herself. I hold up one of my shoes. "Does it look like I'm stalking?"

She grins and tilts her head. Her shiny black hair slides across her face. I'd like to touch that hair. "So what are you doing here?" she asks.

I've recovered enough to say something intelligent. "We'd all like to know the answer to that question, wouldn't we? The best minds on the planet have been considering that very thing since the dawn of life."

"I doubt it."

"Come on. That's the big question of existence."

"Yeah, but since the dawn of life?" she says. "I don't think single-celled organisms were asking what they're doing here. Besides, you know that's not what I meant. I want to know what you're doing sitting in front of my house."

"Huh?" I say again. I look around. The house behind me doesn't have the right address. But the house almost straight across the street does. Figures. Stop paying attention for five minutes and *wham*. The universe gets you. Why is it that any flukes being handed out are never in my favor? I keep my eyes wandering, then shrug and try to sound bored. "So which place is yours?"

She points. "That one. Are you telling me you didn't know?"

"Why would I know that?"

"Hmm," she says. "Okay. Maybe you can tell me why you took your shoes off."

I shake my head. "Sorry. That information is top secret."

She considers this for a moment, keeps watching me with her blue eyes. She looks disappointed. Finally she mutters, "Fine." And she starts walking.

"Wait!" I scramble to my feet, start hopping up and down, trying to get a shoe back on.

She stops.

"I was just trying to see how they're made."

Rowan looks back and it's hard to read her expression. "Why?"

I'm nervous now. Or should I say more nervous? I have the feeling that my answer is important. I think about making something up, like I'm planning to be a shoe designer when I get out of school. But a trace of impatience shows on her face and I blurt out the truth. "Because of the kids in the factories. I was trying to understand what it feels like, making shoes all day."

"Really?" she says.

"Yeah."

She walks back and does that head-tilting, hair-sliding thing again. Then she nods. "I've thought about that too. It must be harsh."

"For sure." I want to say more, but my mind is totally blank.

She sighs. "Well, I've got to get going. I guess I'll see you at the battle next week?"

"Yeah. We'll be there."

"Good." She gets this wicked gleam in her eye and says, "We could use a little competition." Then she turns and saunters off. She doesn't look like she's in any hurry.

A hundred things I want to say flash through my mind, but none of them makes it out of my mouth. I just stand there and watch her go. And then I know exactly what I want to write a song about. Desire.

I don't get too far with this. I sit down to put my shoes back on. When I stand up to go home, there's Amy on the other side of the street, smirking. All the dizzy fizzy feelings I wanted to hold on to and try to put into words just vanish. That girl really creeps me out.

Chapter Nine

Our final practice before the battle doesn't go well. We can't get in sync. Every time we start a number, one of us blows it. Cia screws up the fill or Kel loses the bass line or I mess up the lyrics. All three of us are getting edgy, and when we go down for about the tenth time, I've had enough.

"This is useless. Let's just forget it."

Cia fires one of her sticks across the room and says, "What the hell's your problem, Jay?"

"My problem? Since when is it my problem?"

"Since you want to just quit. What's up with that?"

"Yeah," says Kel. "That sucks."

I look at them glaring at me and I get a very bad feeling. Something about the chemistry in The Lunar Ticks has changed. I set my guitar down and narrow my eyes. "What's going on here?"

They flash each other guilty looks and then Cia says, "What do you mean?"

"I mean something's different. I want to know what it is."

"Hey, man," Kel stutters. "Everything's cool. We're just having a bad day. No need to get all worked up."

"Yeah," Cia says brightly. "I heard it's supposed to be good luck when things go wrong in the dress rehearsal."

I snort. "Good luck? If we play like this on Saturday night, we're going to get booed right off the stage."

"So we keep practicing. Or we have another practice tomorrow night."

"I already told you, I can't practice tomorrow." I don't tell them the reason I can't practice. The full moon.

"But, Jay, this is important!" Cia looks like she wants to hit me with the other stick.

"Tell me something I don't know. Like what else is going on?" I say.

"Man," Kel moans. "It's like this…"

"Kel!" Cia snarls.

"We gotta tell him, Cia."

"Tell me what?" I ask. But I think I already know.

"Well, me and Cia…we're sort of hooked up."

"Hooked up?" I ask.

Cia echoes me. "Hooked up?"

Kel's long face is flushing. "Yeah. Like we're going out or something." He looks sideways at Cia. "Right?"

Cia rolls her eyes.

Suddenly I'm enjoying this. "Is that right?" I drawl. "Since when?"

"Since a couple of days ago," Kel says. He swallows and his Adam's apple bobs up and down. "We were going to tell you after the show."

"Why the secret?" I ask.

Kel swallows again, looks at Cia again. "It wasn't exactly a secret. It's just that we haven't made it official or anything. And we thought we'd see how it goes. You know. Like that."

"Like that, eh?" I say. I cross my arms, crunch down my eyebrows. "I don't know if this is such a good idea. It seems like it might affect our band."

"Yeah," Cia says glumly. "We thought of that."

"And that's why we were waiting," Kel says.

"Right. So you two are all hot for each other and you figured no one would notice?"

Kel looks relieved. "That's right."

I have to ask. "What happens if you get in a fight?"

"Aw, man. We won't get in a fight." Kel seems to actually believe this.

Cia isn't quite as certain. "Look, Jay. We're not stupid. We know it could cause problems. But what are we supposed to do? Pretend it isn't real? Because it is, and I'm not into being phony."

Kel nods his head vigorously. "That's it, Jay. We want to be real."

"Honest?" I ask.

"Yeah. Honest."

I can't argue with that. I just wish I could say the same about me. Like maybe I should admit that I might not be able to write any more songs. I should tell them the truth. And I should tell Rowan the truth, that I want a chance to get to know her. I don't say any of that stuff to them. I don't tell them my next thought either—that somehow Amy knew about their attraction before they did.

Instead I say, "Cool. Don't worry about it. We're still going to kick ass on Saturday night, okay?"

They grin and say okay. They look at each other all goofy and happy. I'm really grateful they don't start making out in front of me. I take off before that can happen. I have some plans to make for tomorrow.

Chapter Ten

Vancouver's Downtown Eastside is not for wusses. It has a scary rep. Drug dealers, prostitutes who disappear, violence. I get off at the nearest Skytrain station, hunch my shoulders and march in.

I head up Main Street and start looking around. This is tricky because I don't want to make eye contact with anyone.

"Say what, hon?" I didn't even notice her sidling up beside me. Maybe she was hiding in the entry too. This girl doesn't look any older than me. Okay, in some ways she doesn't look older. Her body is model thin and she's showing it off in tight clothes. She's wearing lots of makeup, and at first I think she's pretty. But when I make eye contact, I want to take off. Her eyes are empty. That's the only way I can describe it. It's like whoever lived behind those eyes has gone away.

"Um," I mumble, "I guess I was just talking to myself."

She laughs, a high-pitched screech, and says, "We get a lot of that around here, don't we?"

I shrug. "Yeah, I guess."

Her laugh cuts out and she puts a hand on my arm. I catch a whiff of stale perfume and bad breath. She sticks out her tongue and runs it slowly along her red lips, showing off her piercing. "You sure you weren't asking me about doing a little something?"

Oh, man. A hooker. "No. I mean yes. I'm sure."

She pouts and tightens her grip. "I don't understand. Are you saying you don't want me?"

I try shaking her off. "Yeah, that's right."

She puts her face up to mine and hisses, "You think I'm not good enough?" She tosses back her hair and sneers. "Not so long ago I was a perfect little high school student living at home with Mom and Dad. Just like you, right?"

I don't know why, but I feel stung. It's like she's gloating about how much more she knows than me. I say, "So?"

"So why don't you try having some fun? Didn't you say you wanted to get a life?"

I pull my arm away. "Maybe that's not my idea of fun, okay? Maybe *you* should get a life."

Her flat eyes stare at me and something awakens there. It looks like pain. She says, "I did have a life."

I want to ask her what happened, but I think I can guess. Instead I ask, "Can't you go back?"

She looks at me like I just grew a third arm, and her eyes are empty again. "As if."

"Are you sure? I mean, can't you…"

"Oh, shut up! What do you know, baby boy?" And she totters away. The sharp click of her spike heels sounds like teeth chattering.

Baby boy.

She's right. What do I know? I'm a fake. This is retarded. It's not going to turn me into a creative genius. I'm just a stupid regular guy from the stupid burbs, and hanging around here is not going to change that. Not. I bolt for the Skytrain. I swear I hear her laughter following me.

I ride the train back with the full moon looking down at me, and the taste in my mouth is bitter. What now? Do I give up on The Lunar Ticks? I make a deal with myself. I'm not going to let down Kel and Cia, so tomorrow night we compete. If we win, then there's no problem. If we lose...then maybe it's time to put our little band on hold while I take the five bucks and go.

An image of Rowan pops into my head. Indigo Daze could beat us for sure, but that's not why I'm thinking about her. I'm thinking it's time I did something about her too. No more baby boy.

I stare out into the darkness and see my face reflected in the glass. I look like a ghost flying along out there, pale and spooky. Spying on the world.

Chapter Eleven

Five bands are playing in the battle and The Lunar Ticks have drawn the fourth play slot. Indigo Daze is fifth. All of the musicians are supposed to report to the show manager before the battle starts. My dad drives our van around the building to the back entrance so we can unload our instruments. As we drive past the crowd waiting out front, some of the kids yell out our names and cheer. This makes me feel a lot better, like maybe I am for real.

But as we haul our gear into the back room, I can tell something is wrong. The other musicians waiting inside are too quiet.

"Isn't that him?" someone says.

I look in the direction of the voice and recognize the drummer from Indigo Daze. He's staring at me like he wants to rip my face off. I flick a glance around the room and everyone's watching me.

"Whassup?" Cia whispers.

"I dunno," I answer.

"Scumbag." It's the drummer again.

"What is your problem, man?" I ask.

And then I see Rowan, hunched down on the floor behind him. She grabs his sleeve and says, "Stop it. We don't know it was him."

The drummer ignores her, keeps his eyes pinned on me. "You're my problem," he sneers. "And you know why."

"What are you talking about?" I ask.

"Yeah," Kel says, backing me up. He opens his mouth to say more, but before he can, the drummer reaches down and grabs a guitar. It's a Gibson Firebird and it's all smashed up.

"Jeez," I say. I'm pretty sure it's Rowan's guitar. "What happened?"

"You're saying you don't know?" He shakes the guitar at me.

"What? How would I know?"

"Because you know where Rowan lives. You were at her house the other day for no reason. And last night someone broke into her garage and did this. Maybe you just don't want to lose tonight, eh?"

The mood in the room is ugly. No one moves, but it feels like everyone there, including the other band members, has taken a step toward me. I feel boxed in and scan their faces for sympathy. Not everyone looks like they want to pound me, but most of them do.

I glance at Kel and he's gawking at me with his eyes bugging out. I can almost see what he's thinking. I didn't want to have band practice last night. And I asked him to cover for me again while I did my moon thing. I think I even said some stuff about how I was sure we could beat Indigo Daze. Could he really believe I trashed Rowan's guitar? Cia looks angry. Her spiky hair is quivering and her nostrils are pinched like she just came across a bad smell.

I look at them but speak loud enough for everyone to hear. "Just because I know where someone lives doesn't mean anything. I wouldn't do something that low."

Slowly, Kel nods. "Yeah," he says. "That's right. Jay would never wreck a guitar. Never."

Kel doesn't stop there. He blurts, "Besides, Jay was with me last night." Kel shouldn't have kept talking. He's a lousy liar.

"Are you sure about that, dude?" the drummer asks. "Cuz you don't look too sure."

"Yeah, I'm sure," Kel says angrily. But he turns away and drops his eyes to the floor. Cia shoots her dark eyes from him to me and back again. Then she bites down on her lip and crosses her arms.

I ignore the drummer and focus on Rowan. "Did you call the cops? Maybe they know who did it."

"Oh yeah," the drummer scoffs. "Rowan reported it." This guy's like a dog with a bone. No way he's letting go.

"But the cops didn't even bother to come out. They just gave her a number and that was it."

A mutter goes around the room. I shake my head. I can feel sweat beading on my neck and resist the urge to run out into the cool evening. This whole scene feels surreal, like there's no way this should be happening. But I can't figure out what to say next. How do I convince them it wasn't me?

I get a reprieve from the show manager. He throws open the stage door and hustles into the room. Then we hear crowd noise building. They must have opened the outside doors, and the youth center is filling up fast. Some of the audience is already stamping and hooting, impatient for the show to start. The manager is focused on a clipboard. "I'll get the rest of you checked in soon. Fat Roaches? You here?"

A group steps forward and the manager nods. "Let's go, then. You're on." The group shares a few high fives and follows him out to the stage. A minute later a warm-up riff comes howling out of an amp, and the focus of the room shifts away from me. Other groups start picking up their instruments and checking them out. Kel grabs my arm and yanks me aside. He puts his mouth to my ear and hisses, "Where were you last night, man?"

I shake my head. "I can't tell you. But I can tell you this. I sure as hell didn't smash up anyone's guitar."

He presses his lips tight together and nods sharply. "Okay. I guess I believe you, man."

"You guess?" I ask him.

He gestures impatiently. "I do. But this doesn't look good, you know?"

What can I say? He's right. Cia comes and stands next to us and we huddle together, keep our distance from the other players. I keep looking over at Rowan, but she never even glances in my direction.

When the show manager hurries back into the room, he runs his finger over his clipboard and yells, "Lunar Ticks? Are you guys here?"

I call out, "Yeah, we're here."

"Okay, so the only ones I haven't got checked in yet are Indigo Daze."

Indigo's drummer waves him over. "That's us. But we're withdrawing from the battle."

"Huh? Why?"

The drummer points to Rowan's guitar. "Technical problem."

The manager gapes at the guitar and blurts, "No kidding." Then everyone is looking my way again.

"How about this?" I say. "She can use my guitar."

Finally Rowan lifts her head. I keep talking. "Mine's a Gibson too. It shouldn't feel too weird for you."

"Are you serious?" she asks.

"Absolutely."

The drummer laughs. "Nice try, man. Guilty conscience bothering you?"

"No! I just don't think it's fair if you guys don't get your chance. That's it. No big deal."

Rowan stands up and walks toward me. "You know," she says softly, "if we get to play, we're going to win."

Cia's chin comes up and she says, "I wouldn't be too sure about that if I were you."

Rowan looks at Cia and smiles. "You're Lunar's drummer, aren't you? You're good, real good."

The smile is friendly and Cia can't help herself. She grins back. "Thanks." And right there it's like someone opened a window in a smoky room and the air starts clearing. *Whoosh*. I start breathing more easily.

I reach out and touch Rowan's shoulder. "It wasn't me, okay?"

Her eyes search mine and after a long moment she nods. "Okay."

I could keep looking into those eyes for a lot longer, but I don't. Instead I turn, pick up my Gibson and offer it to her. "Here. Check it out."

Rowan takes the guitar, holds it flat to check the balance, slides her hands up and down the neck. "Hmm. It feels a bit different, but I think I can work with it."

"Good. But just so you know, The Lunar Ticks are going to win."

"No way," she scoffs.

"Way," I say. This is more like it.

Chapter Twelve

When we get out there, we're still kinda rattled. We're halfway through the first number before it feels like we're really in sync. But then it's as if we channel all of our mixed-up feelings into the music and things get better. The music vibrates around us like an electrical storm and we keep going. The crowd gets into it and we feed off them, push ourselves hard.

I see Amy out in front as usual, and she has her beady eyes fixed on Kel. I don't think he looks her way once, even when she keeps yelling his name.

The crowd pours on the applause after we're done, so we stay out there, soaking it up. Then the manager's voice is in my ear and he says, "We're on a schedule here. Come on, the next group is already onstage."

Sure enough, Indigo Daze is walking on, but Rowan looks hesitant. I know what her problem is. A musician feels naked getting up in front of a crowd without an instrument. I sometimes figure my guitar is like a shield, a nice shiny piece of armor. I pull the strap over my head and hand my Gibson to her.

"Jay! You jerk!" someone screams. "Stop!"

I turn and get a full blast of smoking rage from Amy. "After what

I did for Kel to win, and now you're helping them!" Her eyes widen and she clamps a hand over her mouth. Her big mouth.

I step toward her. "What did you do, Amy?"

Amy's gaze darts wildly, fixes on Kel. He's finally looking at her but he doesn't say a word. He just shakes his head in disgust, takes hold of Cia's hand and walks offstage. I glance over at Rowan and I can tell she's figured it out. Her face is grim, and Indigo's drummer gets it too. He curls his lip and says, "She's gonna pay."

When I look back for Amy, she's gone.

I retreat from the stage, and a minute later we're listening to Indigo Daze.

They're fantastic. They've gone to a higher level, and when Rowan slides into their last number, a new song I've never heard, I know for sure that they've won. I tell myself that kind of talent deserves the win. I refuse to think about my kind of talent. The losing kind.

Everyone backstage is clapping and whistling for them when they come back. Rowan walks up to me and plants a kiss on my cheek. "Thanks," she whispers.

She goes to hand me my guitar but I say, "No. Keep it for now. The winner usually gets to play an encore."

She grins and says, "You think?"

"Oh yeah," I say. "I think." I take a deep breath and add, "But I'm thinking about something else too."

"What?"

"That I'd like to get to know you better."

She tilts her head and the black hair slides and her blue eyes smile. "Sounds nice."

"How about tomorrow? We could go for a walk at the beach. Maybe get some coffee?"

"Okay. Is noon a good time?"

It is.

Chapter Thirteen

It's a real good time. The tide is out and there's plenty of open beach to travel. We talk and talk, and before I know it I'm spilling everything about my full-moon hunts for experience. Rowan stops and stares at me and I think she's going to laugh. But she doesn't. She takes hold of my hand and says, "What's your hurry?"

I shrug. "I know. It's kind of lame, but life moves too slow sometimes. I'm planning to notch things up a bit. Get beyond just spying on the rest of the world."

"Spying on the world. That sounds like a title for a song."

I start to disagree, then stop. Maybe that is a title, but it's not as if I'm going to be writing any more music for a while. I give her a lopsided grin. "How did you get so smart?"

"Me? I'm not smart. I think I'm just wired this way. Almost everything feels like music to me. Sometimes I'd like to turn it off and just be normal, but I can't."

This is unbelievable. "You want to be normal?"

"Don't you?"

"No. I already am and it sucks."

She laughs. "You're not normal."

"I'm not?"

"Not." She ponders for a minute. "I don't think anybody is. There's no such thing as normal. But you—you're less normal than most."

"Jeez," I say. "That's the nicest thing anyone ever said to me. Thanks."

"You're welcome."

We walk a little farther, stop and look out at the blue water. "For me," she says softly, "life sort of sped up. I had a sister who died a while ago. That was hard. Still is. You remind me of her."

A tingle runs down my spine and I almost drop her hand. I remind her of her dead sister? This can't be good. I croak, "Why?"

She keeps her gaze fixed on the horizon, and when she finally talks, her voice seems far away. "She was always looking for that next thrill, you know?"

I don't think she really wants an answer so I just wait.

Rowan takes a breath and talks on. "She was so extreme—with everything. Like, she had hair down to her waist and went for a trim. Came back with it cut above her ears. She'd obsess over some movie star, be so into him. Then she'd see him interviewed on TV and decide he was the biggest turd on the planet."

"Really?" I don't tell her this isn't making any sense to me.

"Yeah, really. No matter what she did, it was all or nothing. She just flew, never stopped to figure anything out."

"And you don't think I bother to figure things out?"

Rowan sighs. "That's not it. I think you are figuring things out. I guess what I see in you is that hunger. That need to fill up on life. I used to envy Willow because she was always so busy. But then I saw that none of it ever satisfied her. She never got into anything, you know? Not anything that meant something to her or made her feel good about herself."

"So what happened to her?"

"Nothing special, Jay. She just went tripping on drugs and never came back."

"You mean she overdosed?"

"Yeah." Her voice cracks as she adds, "Big time."

My gut reacts to this. It sinks, hits bottom and I feel sick. I want to say something to ease Rowan's pain. Only I can't think of anything. I just stand there beside her and hold her hand and look at the water.

"So you get it, right?" she asks.

She's staring at me and I know she wants me to understand something. There's no way I can lie. "Get what?"

She drops my hand, and for a second I think she might hit me. "You don't get what I'm saying? God, I thought for sure you would. Just forget it."

"No. I want to understand. Please." I make a grab to recapture her hand, but she backs away.

"Jay, I don't usually talk about Willow. I only told you because of..." she stops.

"Because of what? Because of my full-moon nights?"

She nods. "Yeah. Because of that. See, I figure if Willow had waited, just given life some time, she would have found something special. Something real. Or it would have found her."

Okay, this is starting to make sense. "Something special. Like music?"

She smiles. "So you do get it!"

"Let me put it this way, I'm trying."

"Yeah? Maybe it would help if I told you why I think you're abnormal?"

I'm not so sure about that, but I act cool and say, "Okay."

She tucks a strand of hair behind her ear and considers. I'm expecting

something really great and she says,
"I think you're different because of that
time you sat down and looked at your
shoes."

Wow. Who'd have thought? I stuff
my hands into my pockets and get this
little jolt when my fingers find the five-
dollar bill, the one from the fridge at
home. I put it in my pocket when I got
home last night. I glance at Rowan and
notice she's expecting an answer.

"Looking at my shoes means what,
exactly?"

"Well, how many people take the
time to really look at things? You go
below the surface, Jay. That's where the
important stuff in life happens."

I stare at her and she waits patiently.
I like this about her, maybe more than
anything else. She's not in a hurry.
I don't want to disappoint her and tell
her I hardly ever look at my shoes.
Instead I take my hand from my pocket

and hold up the bill, show it to Rowan. "See this?"

"Yeah."

"Well this. This is something. It's meant to go somewhere."

"Is that a fact?" she says.

"It is. It's a fact. It goes with a pair of shoes, to take you places."

Her eyes narrow and she studies me closely. "What places?"

"I don't know. Any place you want."

"Special places?" she asks.

I shrug. "How can you tell if a place is special when you haven't even been there yet? Sometimes you have to take chances."

Her lips curve into that little half smile and I'm dying to know what's going through her head. She says, "I'd like to get to know you better too, Jay."

I stand there and blink. Huh? I'm talking about going places and she comes up with that smile and says she wants to get to know me? And then, just like that, it's all clear. The only place I *really* want to go right now is closer to Rowan. Funny how that can happen. Two people talking about two different things, but it's really the same thing if you look at it the right way.

I stare down at the bill in my hand and say, "There are all kinds of trips, right?" Then I hold my hand above my head, letting the bill flutter in the strengthening wind. I let it go and the wind takes it into the water. I see it briefly on the crest of a wave before it disappears below the surface.

Rowan says, "That was strange."

I say, "Why?"

She says, "Because I thought that was for that coffee you promised me and you just had a funny way of getting around to it. What exactly have we been talking about here, Jay?"

Man.

"Oh, you know. You were right. I'm just abnormal."

"Oh really?" She gets that wicked gleam I've seen before, steps sideways and stomps her foot into a tidal pool. Salt water splashes all over me.

"Hey!"

"Gotcha!" she laughs and takes off running.

Of course I chase her. I catch her too and give back as good as I got. By the time we're done we're both soaked, and I haven't felt so good in a long time.

Chapter Fourteen

Kel, Cia and me are in the garage. It's our first time getting together since the battle and it's been a couple of weeks. So far, we're just sitting around, pretending that we're tuning up.

"So," I say.

"Yeah," says Cia.

"Guess who I saw?" Kel asks.

I bite. "Who?"

"Amy. She's working at the new donut joint. Wearing one of those brown dresses."

"No way." I try to picture Amy in the donut dress and it doesn't look good.

"Yeah. She pretended she didn't see me, so I went along with that. But I heard she sort of needs the money."

Cia grins. "Couldn't be for a certain guitar she needs to pay off, could it?"

"Hey," Kel says, "could be."

We laugh but not too loud. It's okay that Amy is putting things right, but somewhere in there I guess we feel sorry for her too. It must suck to be so dumb. But who knows? Maybe after this she'll be smarter. Maybe Amy will know who Amy really is. Or at least she could be figuring it out. Like me.

But what I need to know just now is if The Lunar Ticks know who they are. As in, do we still exist?

"So," I say again. I pluck a string on my guitar, let the sound fade. "What do you think?"

They know what I mean. "Well," Kel says. "I think we were pretty good last time."

"Yeah," Cia agrees, "we were. Just not quite as good as some of the competition."

"That's how I see it too. The question is, will we ever be as good?"

We look at each other. It's down to this. Is it time to call it quits? Or do we still share the dream?

Kel's the first one to speak. "The Fender is still at the music store."

"And final exams are over," Cia says.

Kel and I stare at her.

"Well," she splutters, "they are."

I nod. "So what you're saying is it's too soon to give up? We've got some time?"

"More than that," Cia says. "We've got us. And the music."

"For sure," Kel says. "We just gotta keep paying our dues."

A warm flash of excitement pulses through me. It's still there. I want to do this. "All right then! So, do you wanna hear some new lyrics?"

They grin and lean forward. "Bring it on," Kel says.

"It's called 'Spying on the World'…"

I went out and hid
There in the dark
Tried to look through your eyes
Feel with your heart.
I felt so cold
Like a guy in a lab
Experience,
I wanted you bad.
But here I am
Still just me
Skimming the surface

Won't let me be free
Spying on the world
Living like a fly
Feeding on the crap
Will never take me high
So I'm gonna live
Every day, all the time
And I'm gonna be
Just fine. Just fine.
It's all gonna be
Just fine.

Kel is thoughtful for a while. Then he says, "I like the line about the fly feeding on the crap. My science teacher told us about flies. He said we should keep flies off our food because of what they do. They land on the food and then they barf on it. I think that's to kinda soften it up. Then they walk around in the barf, stirring things up. Finally they eat. Then they poop on the food before they leave."

Cia and I need a moment to consider this information.

"Gross!" Cia decides.

"Yeah, man. That's disgusting," I say.

Kel shrugs. "So? That's the way it is."

I nod. "Okay. I can live with that. Reality as it happens."

"Too right," Kel agrees. He looks at Cia and they smile. Do Rowan and I look that connected when we smile at each other?

"So do you wanna work on this number with me?" I ask. "Get the music part happening?"

"What are you saying?" Cia asks.

"I'm saying that I can't come up with the tune on my own. Got any ideas? Like, what kind of rhythm do we want here? What's the bass going to do?"

Cia's eyes light up and she grabs her sticks. "How about this?" She lays out a pattern, settles down and picks up a beat.

"Yeah. I like that. It feels right. Kel?"

Kel gets intense. He drops his head, closes his eyes, starts false. Then he finds the groove to match Cia. He goes farther and comes up with a sweet undertone. He's echoing Cia, but the bass is alive, making music.

I can feel the grin coming on before it breaks out on my face. "Cool! That sounds good. Real good."

"Jump in any time, Jay," Cia says.

And I do. I connect with the strings and the whole wide world is busy making music.

Acknowledgments

I think fiction writing is very much like making music. It's about arranging words so they flow in harmony, and it requires practice and play. I wish to thank two special authors who enjoy playing with story as much as I do, Shelley Hrdlitschka and Diane Tullson. Their unflagging support is sweet music indeed. My thanks also to Dan Stenning, drummer for the band Rio Bent; his "battle" knowledge is way cool.

K.L. Denman is the popular author of numerous books for youth, including the Governor General's Award nominee *Me, Myself and Ike*. K.L. Denman lives in Powell River, British Columbia.

orca soundings

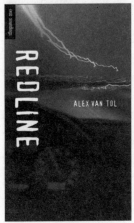

9781554698936 $9.95 PB
9781554698943 $16.95 LIB

Jenessa's a thrill seeker by nature. Anything fast, she's all over it. Angry and blaming herself for her best friend's death, Jenessa escapes to the sanctuary of her car and the freedom of the open road, where she can outrun her memories...if only for a while. She finds a kindred spirit in Dmitri, a warm-hearted speed demon who races at the track. But when Jenessa falls in with a group of street racers—and its irresistible leader, Cody—she finds herself caught up in a web of escalating danger.

orca soundings

9781554699858 $9.95 PB
9781554699865 $16.95 LIB

Bex has explored almost every abandoned building and tunnel in the city. He's into "urban exploration"—going where he's not supposed to go. Bex has always done it just for fun and bragging rights, taking nothing but pictures and leaving nothing but footprints. But that changes when a new kid arrives at school. Kieran is edgy, dangerous and into urban exploration as well. Together, they start pushing each other to radical extremes. When Kieran pitches a plan that involves taking more than just pictures, Bex has a decision to make. Where will he draw the line, and how far will he follow Kieran?

orca soundings

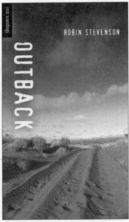

9781554694198 $9.95 PB
9781554694204 $16.95 LIB

Since his girlfriend dumped him, Jayden has been avoiding school-and life in general. When his eccentric uncle Mel invites him to help with his biology research at an Australian university, he figures he has nothing to lose. Once he arrives, he discovers Mel is obsessed with finding a new species of lizard and is determined to be the first to discover it. Unfortunately, this means an expedition into the scorching desert heat of the Australian outback...with the increasingly paranoid Mel and an unfriendly biology student named Natalie. Then disaster strikes, and Jayden and Nat find themselves many miles from civilization fighting for their survival.

Titles in the Series

orca soundings

orca soundings

For more information on all the books
in the Orca Soundings series, please visit
www.orcabook.com.